STAR WARS

IN THE SHADOW OF YAVIN
VOLUME THREE

Since their victory over the Death Star, the Rebel Alliance has been searching for a permanent home base and fighting off attacks by the Empire. Suspecting a spy has been revealing their movements to the enemy, Princess Leia gathers a team of trusted, skilled pilots for a secret mission: find a new base—and uncover the spy.

To resupply the Rebel fleet, Mon Mothma sends smuggler Han Solo and his first mate, Chewbacca, on a secret mission of their own—to Coruscant, the heart of the Empire.

Meanwhile, Darth Vader, suffering the Emperor's scorn after the loss of the Death Star, has been diverted from the pursuit of the Rebels and sent to a remote location . . .

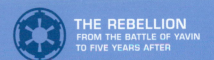

THE REBELLION
FROM THE BATTLE OF YAVIN
TO FIVE YEARS AFTER

The events in this story take place shortly after the events in *Star Wars: Episode IV—A New Hope*.

SCRIPT
BRIAN WOOD

ART
CARLOS D'ANDA

COLORS
GABE ELTAEB

LETTERING
MICHAEL HEISLER

COVER ART
ALEX ROSS

WWW.ABDOPUBLISHING.COM

Reinforced library bound edition published in 2015 by Spotlight, a division of ABDO PO Box 398166, Minneapolis, Minnesota 55439. Spotlight produces high-quality reinforced library bound editions for schools and libraries. Published by agreement with Dark Horse Comics, Inc., and Lucasfilm Ltd.

Printed in the United States of America, North Mankato, Minnesota.
052014
072014

THIS BOOK CONTAINS RECYCLED MATERIALS

LIBRARY OF CONGRESS CATALOGING-IN-PUBLICATION DATA

Wood, Brian, 1972-
    Star Wars : in the shadow of Yavin / writer: Brian Wood ; artist: Carlos D'Anda. -- Reinforced library bound edition.
        pages cm.
    "Dark Horse."
    "LucasFilm."
    ISBN 978-1-61479-286-4 (vol. 1) -- ISBN 978-1-61479-287-1 (vol. 2) -- ISBN 978-1-61479-288-8 (vol. 3) -- ISBN 978-1-61479-289-5 (vol. 4) -- ISBN 978-1-61479-290-1 (vol. 5) -- ISBN 978-1-61479-291-8 (vol. 6)
    1. Graphic novels. I. D'Anda, Carlos, illustrator. II. Dark Horse Comics. III. Lucasfilm, Ltd. IV. Title. V. Title: In the shadow of Yavin.
    PZ7.7.W65St 2015
    741.5'973--dc23

                                    2014005383

Spotlight

A Division of ABDO
www.abdopublishing.com

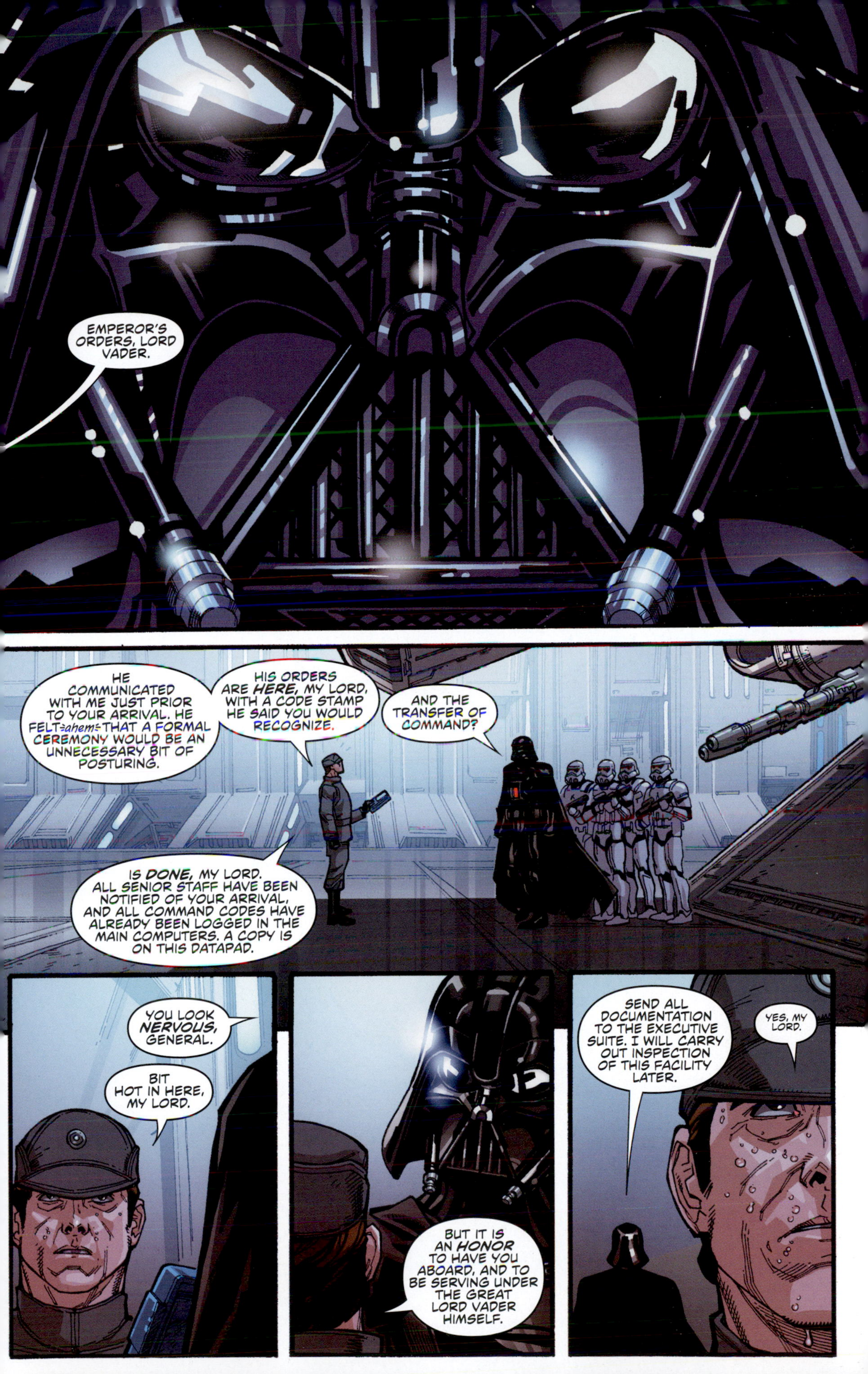
EMPEROR'S ORDERS, LORD VADER.
HE COMMUNICATED WITH ME JUST PRIOR TO YOUR ARRIVAL. HE FELT=ahem=THAT A FORMAL CEREMONY WOULD BE AN UNNECESSARY BIT OF POSTURING.
HIS ORDERS ARE HERE, MY LORD, WITH A CODE STAMP HE SAID YOU WOULD RECOGNIZE.
AND THE TRANSFER OF COMMAND?
IS DONE, MY LORD. ALL SENIOR STAFF HAVE BEEN NOTIFIED OF YOUR ARRIVAL, AND ALL COMMAND CODES HAVE ALREADY BEEN LOGGED IN THE MAIN COMPUTERS. A COPY IS ON THIS DATAPAD.
YOU LOOK NERVOUS, GENERAL.
BIT HOT IN HERE, MY LORD.
BUT IT IS AN HONOR TO HAVE YOU ABOARD, AND TO BE SERVING UNDER THE GREAT LORD VADER HIMSELF.
SEND ALL DOCUMENTATION TO THE EXECUTIVE SUITE. I WILL CARRY OUT INSPECTION OF THIS FACILITY LATER.
YES, MY LORD.

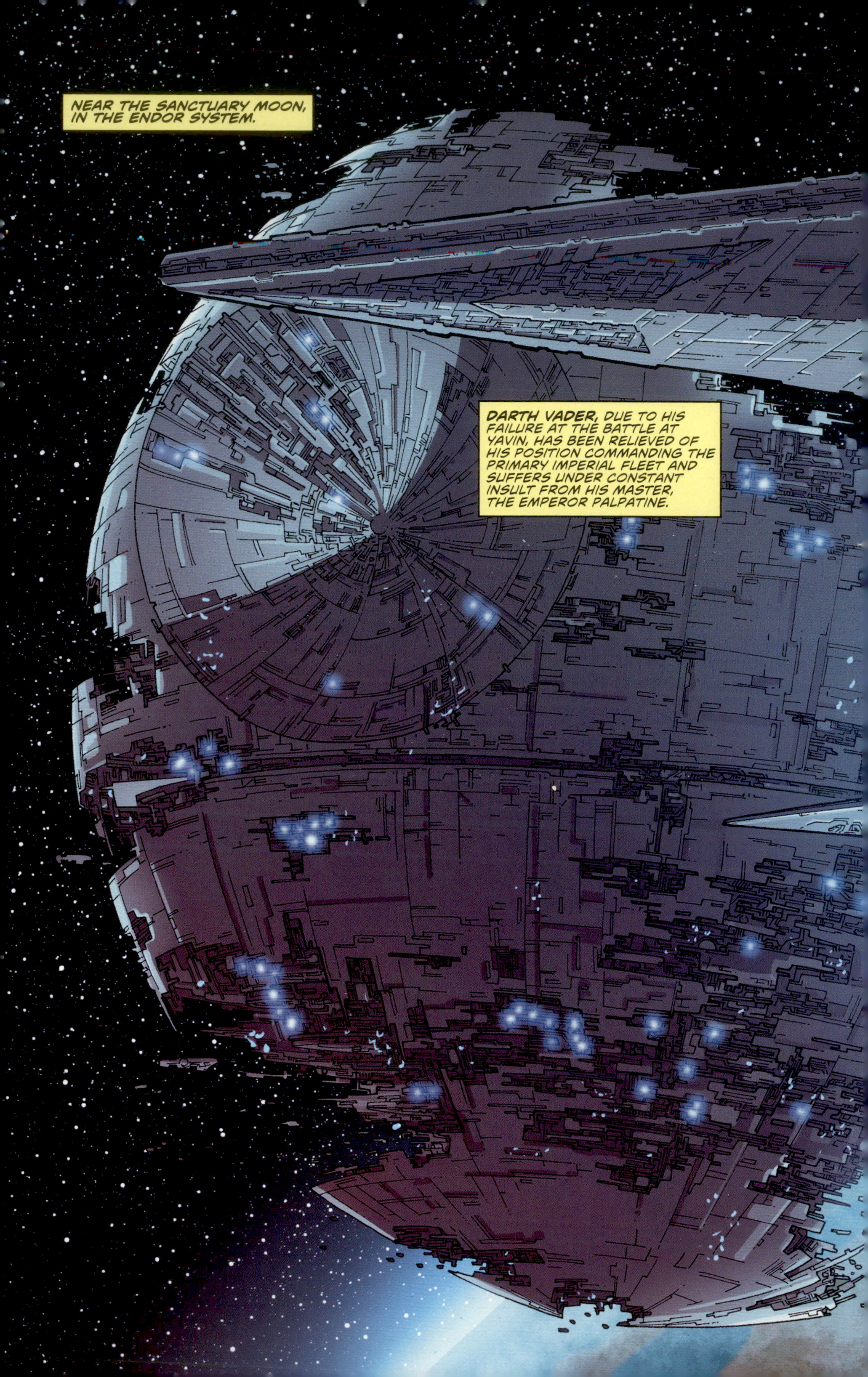
NEAR THE SANCTUARY MOON, IN THE ENDOR SYSTEM.
DARTH VADER, DUE TO HIS FAILURE AT THE BATTLE AT YAVIN, HAS BEEN RELIEVED OF HIS POSITION COMMANDING THE PRIMARY IMPERIAL FLEET AND SUFFERS UNDER CONSTANT INSULT FROM HIS MASTER, THE EMPEROR PALPATINE.

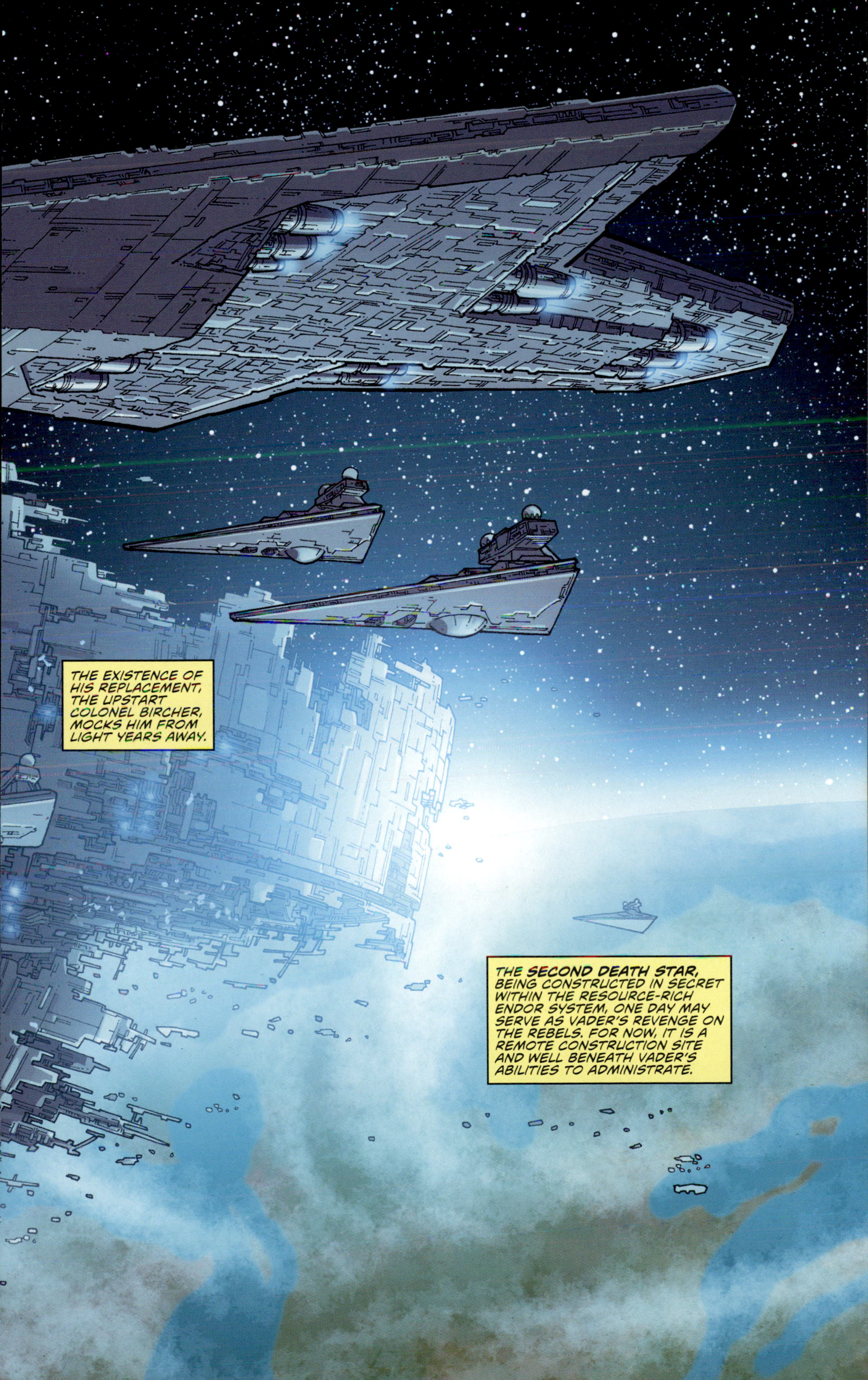
THE EXISTENCE OF HIS REPLACEMENT, THE UPSTART COLONEL BIRCHER, MOCKS HIM FROM LIGHT YEARS AWAY.
THE SECOND DEATH STAR, BEING CONSTRUCTED IN SECRET WITHIN THE RESOURCE-RICH ENDOR SYSTEM, ONE DAY MAY SERVE AS VADER'S REVENGE ON THE REBELS. FOR NOW, IT IS A REMOTE CONSTRUCTION SITE AND WELL BENEATH VADER'S ABILITIES TO ADMINISTRATE.

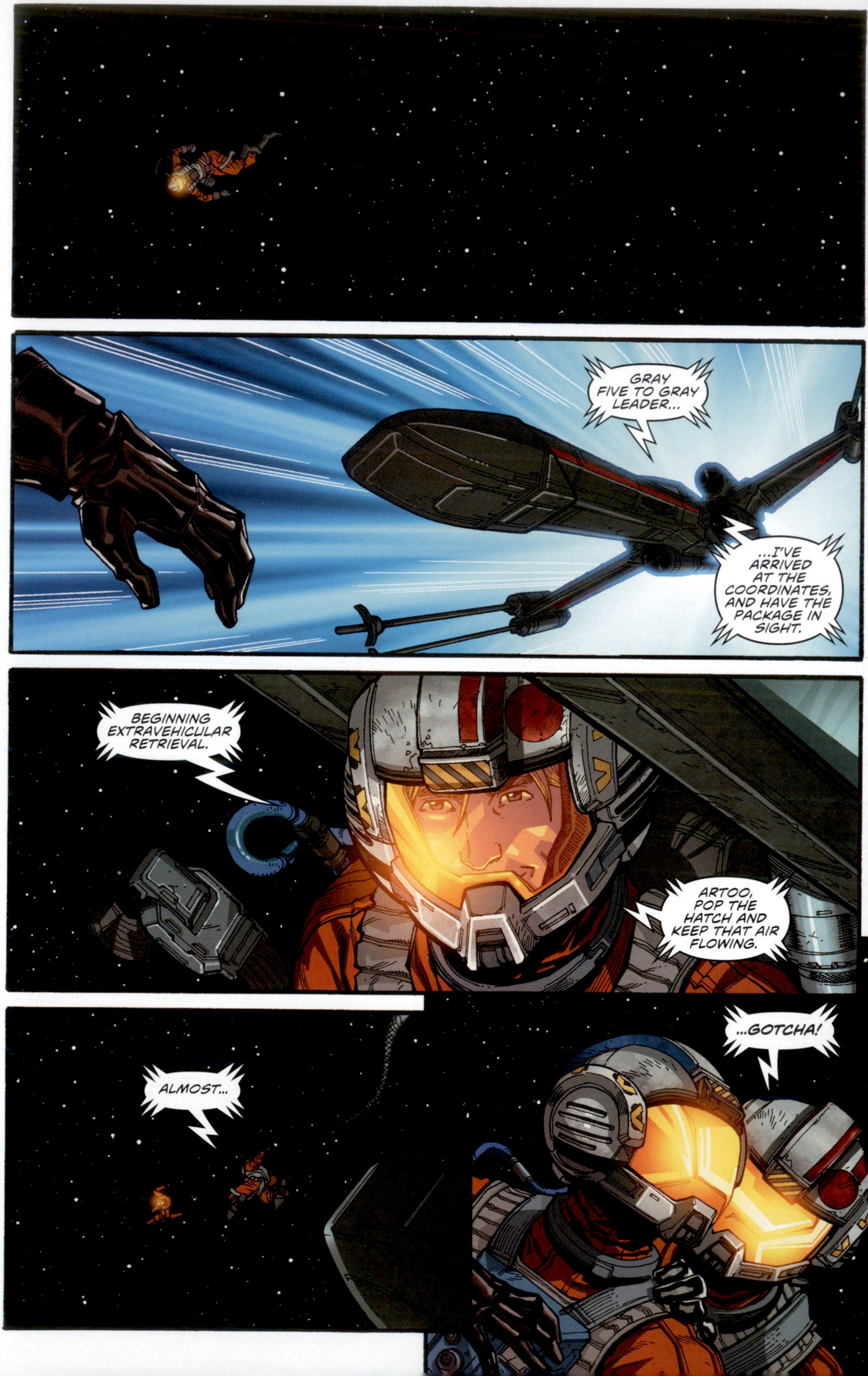
GRAY FIVE TO GRAY LEADER...
...I'VE ARRIVED AT THE COORDINATES, AND HAVE THE PACKAGE IN SIGHT.
BEGINNING EXTRAVEHICULAR RETRIEVAL.
ARTOO, POP THE HATCH AND KEEP THAT AIR FLOWING.
ALMOST...
...GOTCHA!

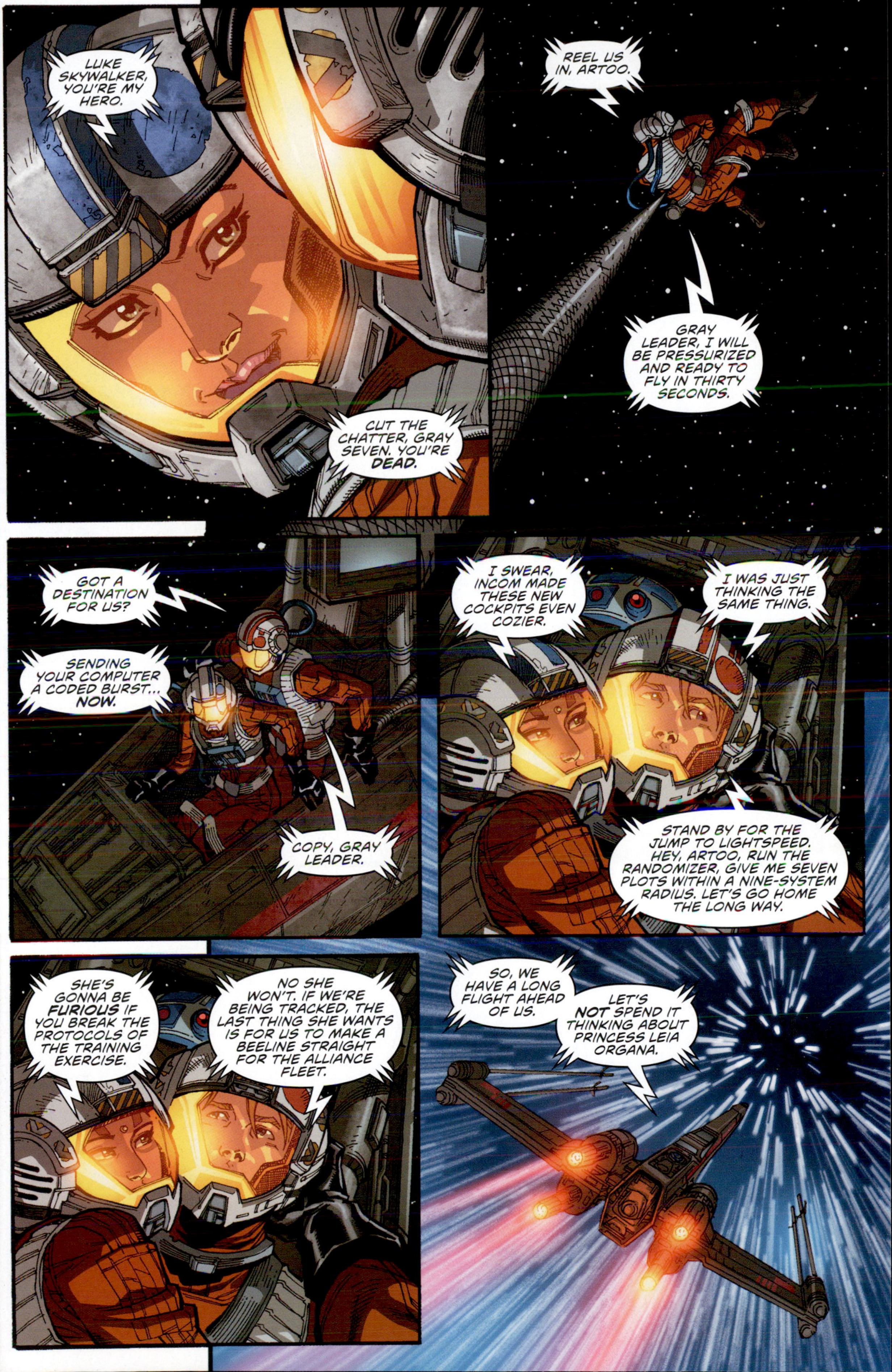
LUKE SKYWALKER, YOU'RE MY HERO.
CUT THE CHATTER, GRAY SEVEN. YOU'RE **DEAD.**
REEL US IN, ARTOO.
GRAY LEADER, I WILL BE PRESSURIZED AND READY TO FLY IN THIRTY SECONDS.
GOT A DESTINATION FOR US?
SENDING YOUR COMPUTER A CODED BURST... **NOW.**
COPY, GRAY LEADER.
I SWEAR, INCOM MADE THESE NEW COCKPITS EVEN COZIER.
I WAS JUST THINKING THE SAME THING.
STAND BY FOR THE JUMP TO LIGHTSPEED. HEY, ARTOO, RUN THE RANDOMIZER, GIVE ME SEVEN PLOTS WITHIN A NINE-SYSTEM RADIUS. LET'S GO HOME THE LONG WAY.
SHE'S GONNA BE **FURIOUS** IF YOU BREAK THE PROTOCOLS OF THE TRAINING EXERCISE.
NO SHE WON'T. IF WE'RE BEING TRACKED, THE LAST THING SHE WANTS IS FOR US TO MAKE A BEELINE STRAIGHT FOR THE ALLIANCE FLEET.
SO, WE HAVE A LONG FLIGHT AHEAD OF US.
LET'S **NOT** SPEND IT THINKING ABOUT PRINCESS LEIA ORGANA.

THE REBEL FLEET,
SOME TIME LATER...

FLIGHT OFFICER
SKYWALKER!

WHERE HAVE YOU BEEN? YOU ARE HOURS OVERDUE.

PRITHI, CONFINE YOURSELF TO QUARTERS UNTIL FURTHER NOTICE.

YES, MA'AM.

LUKE, IN MY BRIEFING ROOM, RIGHT NOW.

BYE.

I'LL FIND YOU LATER.

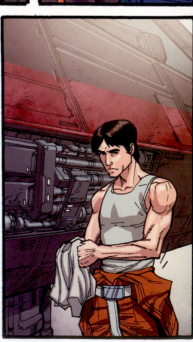

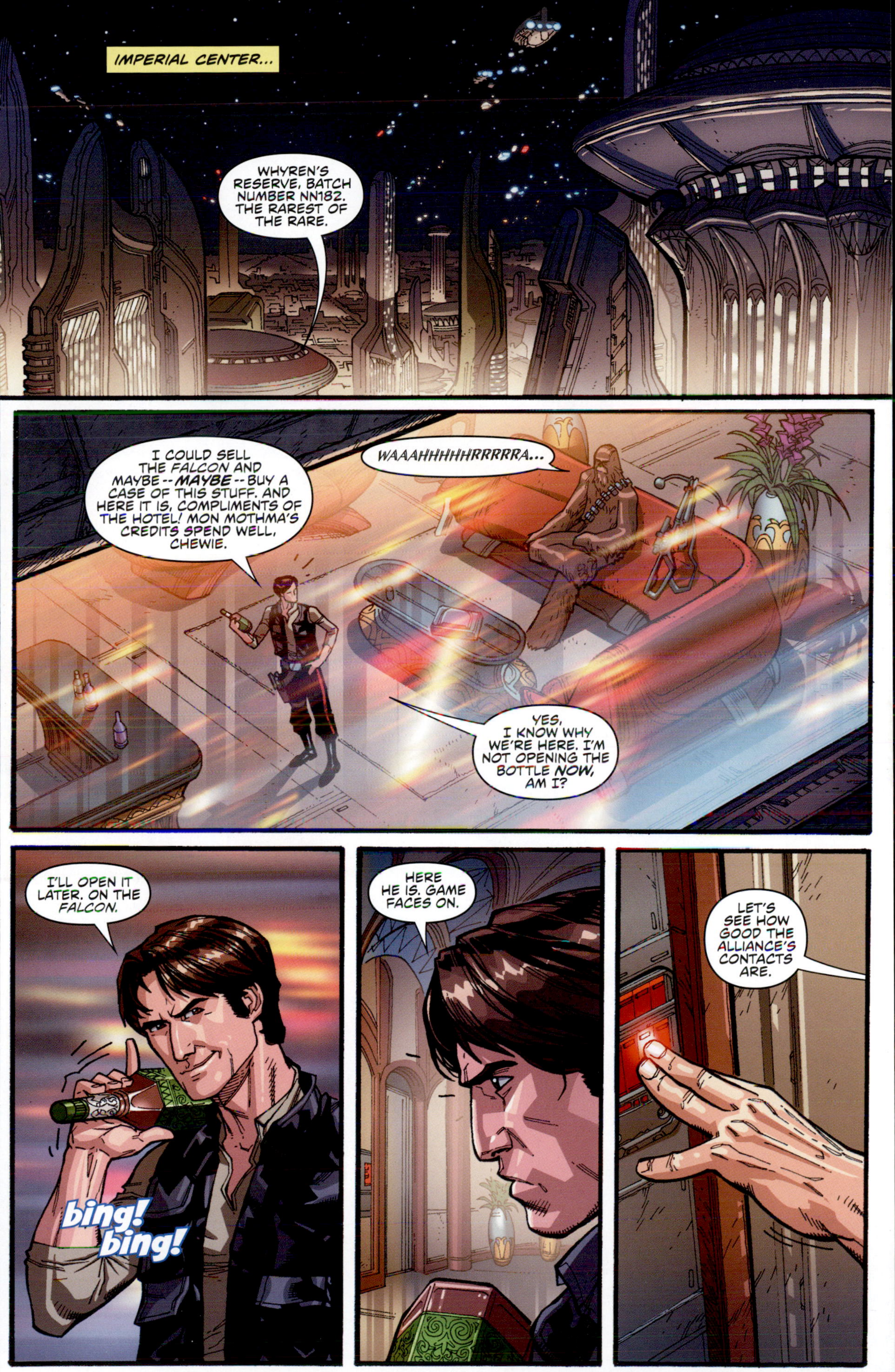
IMPERIAL CENTER...
WHYREN'S RESERVE, BATCH NUMBER NN182. THE RAREST OF THE RARE.
I COULD SELL THE FALCON AND MAYBE--MAYBE--BUY A CASE OF THIS STUFF. AND HERE IT IS, COMPLIMENTS OF THE HOTEL! MON MOTHMA'S CREDITS SPEND WELL, CHEWIE.
WAAAHHHHHRRRRRA...
YES, I KNOW WHY WE'RE HERE. I'M NOT OPENING THE BOTTLE NOW, AM I?
I'LL OPEN IT LATER. ON THE FALCON.
bing! bing!
HERE HE IS. GAME FACES ON.
LET'S SEE HOW GOOD THE ALLIANCE'S CONTACTS ARE.

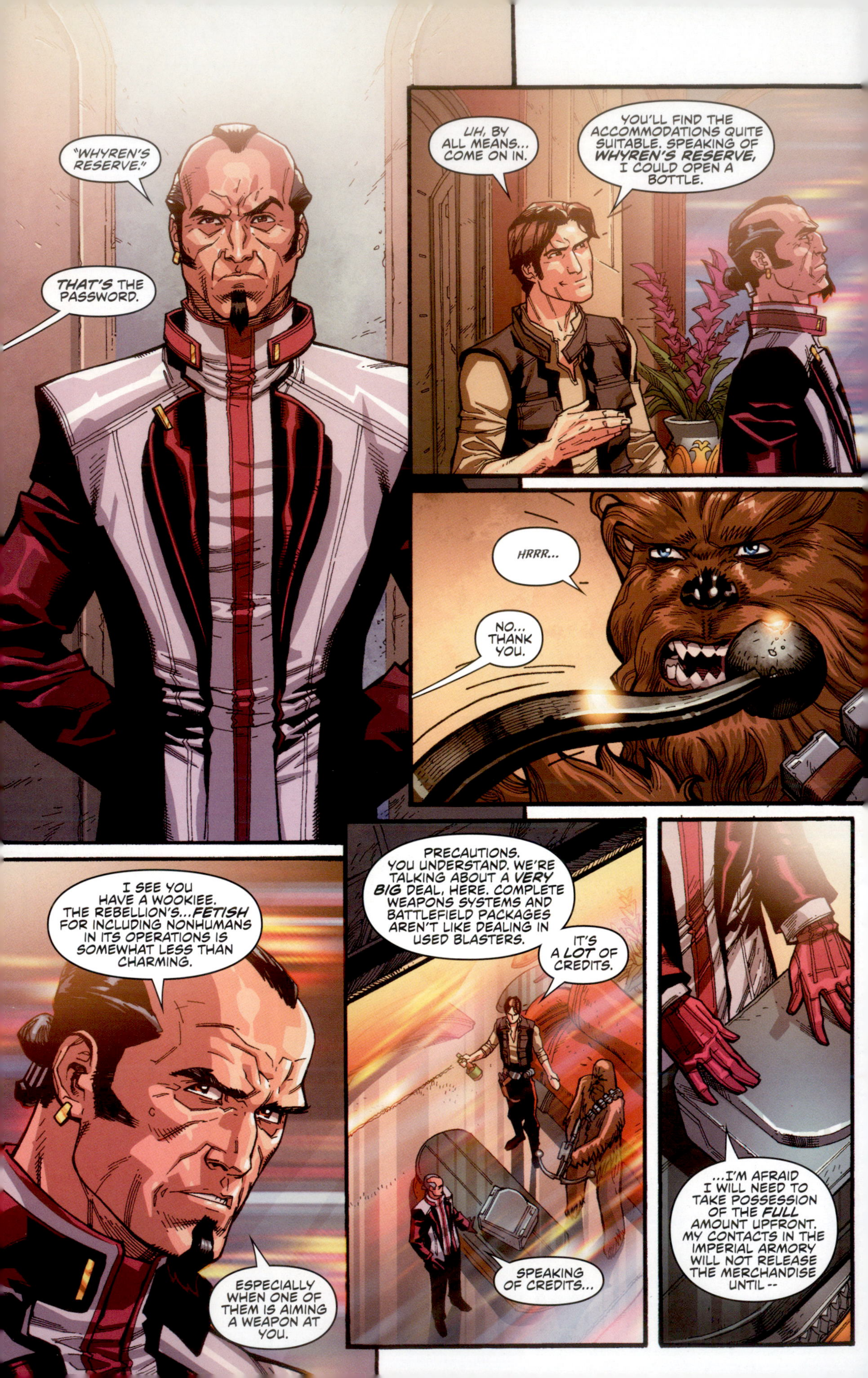
"WHYREN'S RESERVE."
THAT'S THE PASSWORD.
UH, BY ALL MEANS... COME ON IN.
YOU'LL FIND THE ACCOMMODATIONS QUITE SUITABLE. SPEAKING OF *WHYREN'S RESERVE,* I COULD OPEN A BOTTLE.
HRRR...
NO... THANK YOU.
I SEE YOU HAVE A WOOKIEE. THE REBELLION'S...*FETISH* FOR INCLUDING NONHUMANS IN ITS OPERATIONS IS SOMEWHAT LESS THAN CHARMING.
ESPECIALLY WHEN ONE OF THEM IS AIMING A WEAPON AT YOU.
PRECAUTIONS. YOU UNDERSTAND. WE'RE TALKING ABOUT A *VERY BIG* DEAL, HERE. COMPLETE WEAPONS SYSTEMS AND BATTLEFIELD PACKAGES AREN'T LIKE DEALING IN USED BLASTERS.
IT'S A *LOT* OF CREDITS.
SPEAKING OF CREDITS...
...I'M AFRAID I WILL NEED TO TAKE POSSESSION OF THE *FULL* AMOUNT UPFRONT. MY CONTACTS IN THE IMPERIAL ARMORY WILL NOT RELEASE THE MERCHANDISE UNTIL --

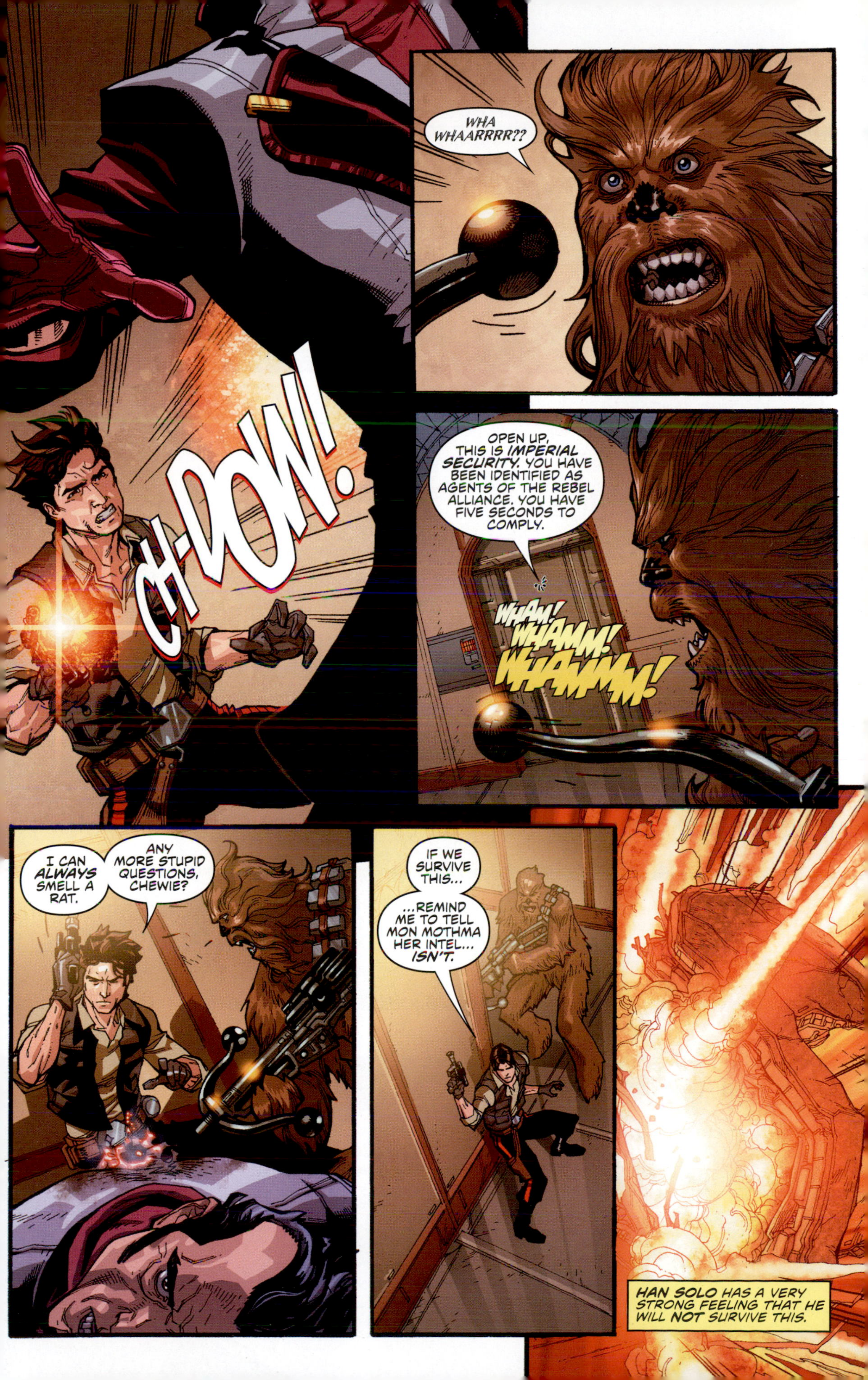
WHA WHAARRRR??
CH-DOW!
OPEN UP, THIS IS IMPERIAL SECURITY. YOU HAVE BEEN IDENTIFIED AS AGENTS OF THE REBEL ALLIANCE. YOU HAVE FIVE SECONDS TO COMPLY.
WHAM! WHAMM! WHAMMM!
I CAN ALWAYS SMELL A RAT.
ANY MORE STUPID QUESTIONS, CHEWIE?
IF WE SURVIVE THIS...
...REMIND ME TO TELL MON MOTHMA HER INTEL... ISN'T.
HAN SOLO HAS A VERY STRONG FEELING THAT HE WILL NOT SURVIVE THIS.

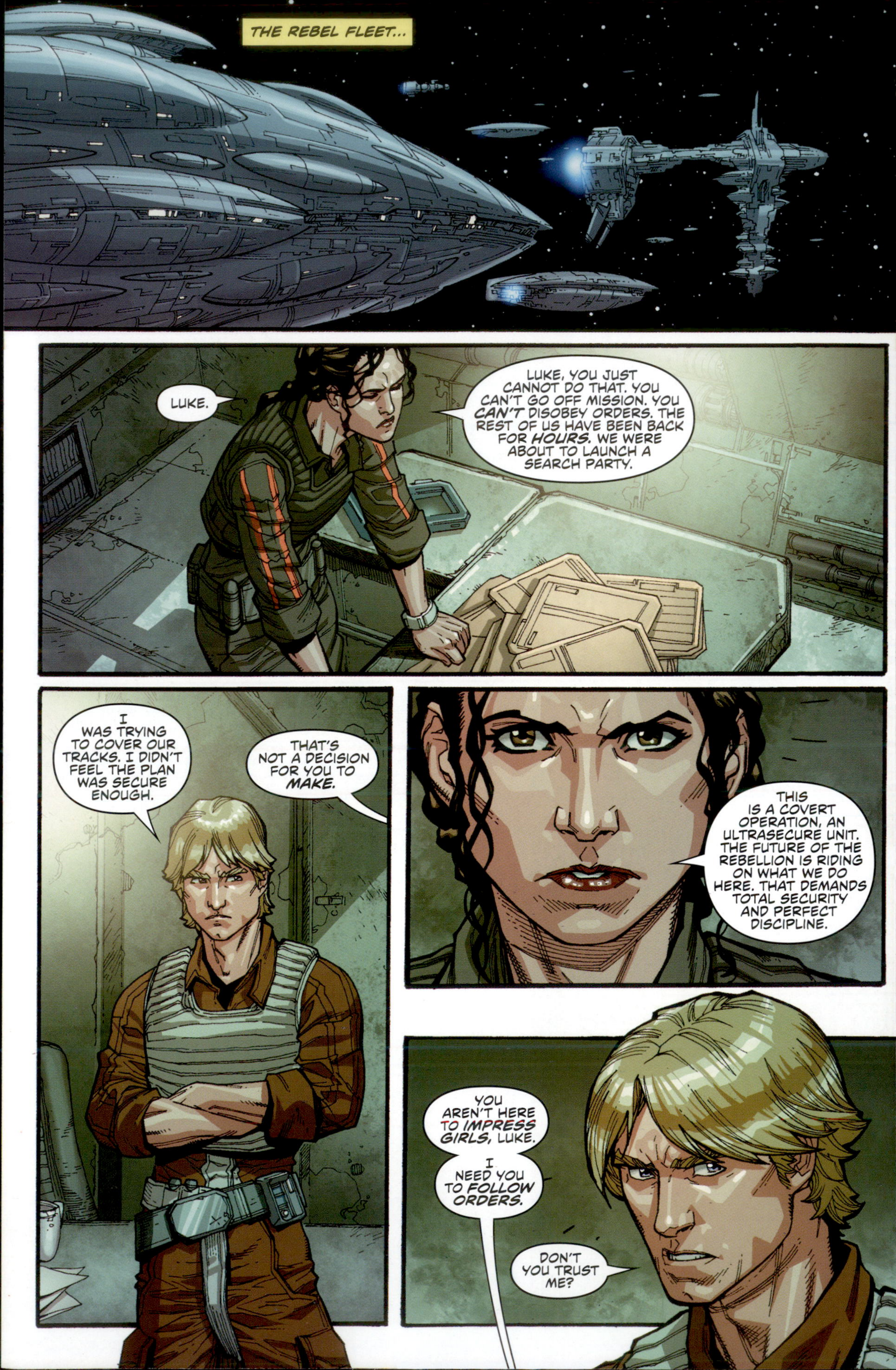
THE REBEL FLEET...
LUKE.
LUKE, YOU JUST CANNOT DO THAT. YOU CAN'T GO OFF MISSION. YOU *CAN'T* DISOBEY ORDERS. THE REST OF US HAVE BEEN BACK FOR *HOURS.* WE WERE ABOUT TO LAUNCH A SEARCH PARTY.
I WAS TRYING TO COVER OUR TRACKS. I DIDN'T FEEL THE PLAN WAS SECURE ENOUGH.
THAT'S NOT A DECISION FOR YOU TO *MAKE.*
THIS IS A COVERT OPERATION, AN ULTRASECURE UNIT. THE FUTURE OF THE REBELLION IS RIDING ON WHAT WE DO HERE. THAT DEMANDS TOTAL SECURITY AND PERFECT DISCIPLINE.
YOU AREN'T HERE TO *IMPRESS GIRLS,* LUKE.
I NEED YOU TO *FOLLOW ORDERS.*
DON'T YOU TRUST ME?

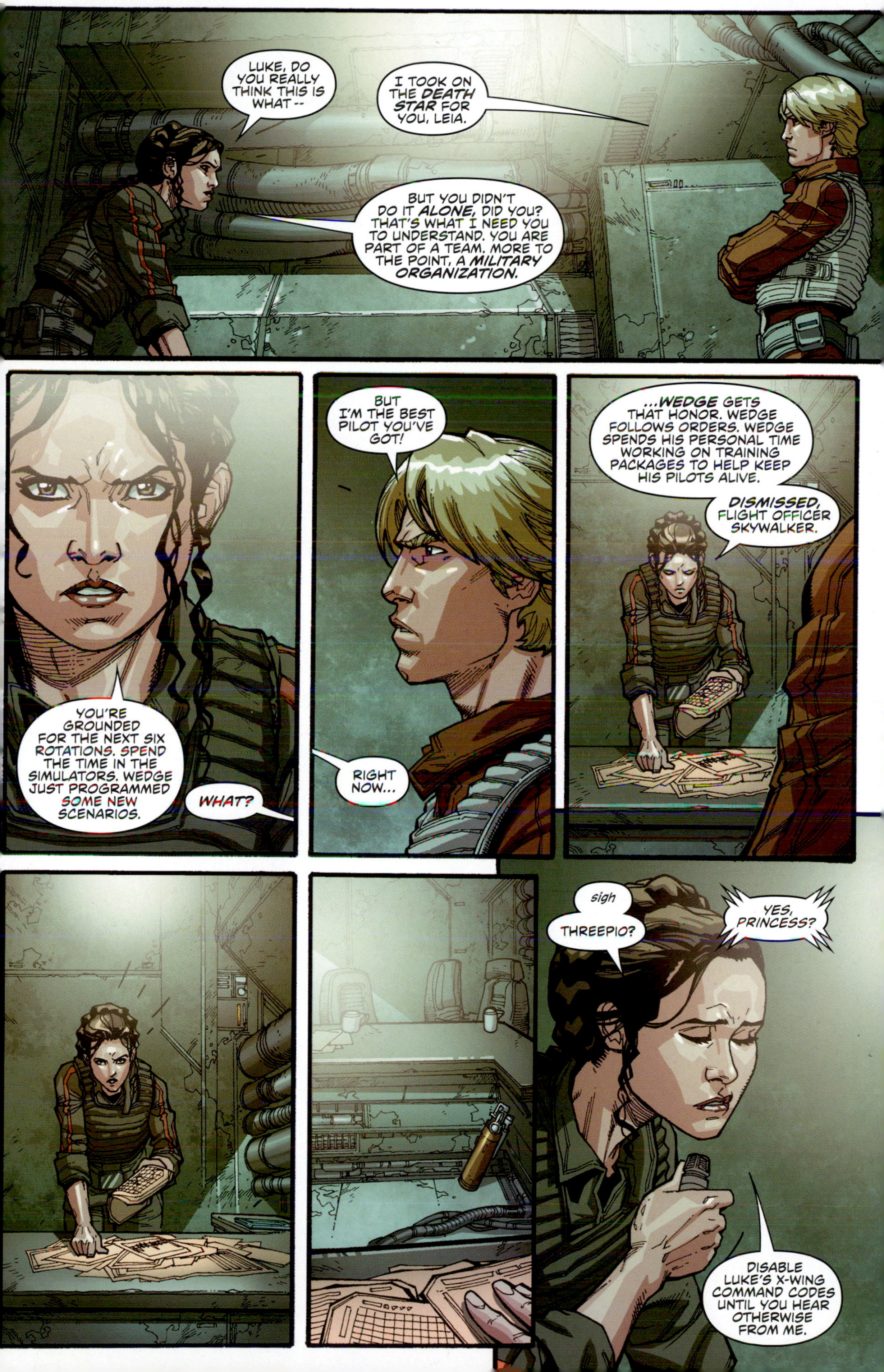
LUKE, DO YOU REALLY THINK THIS IS WHAT --
I TOOK ON THE DEATH STAR FOR YOU, LEIA.
BUT YOU DIDN'T DO IT ALONE, DID YOU? THAT'S WHAT I NEED YOU TO UNDERSTAND. YOU ARE PART OF A TEAM. MORE TO THE POINT, A MILITARY ORGANIZATION.
YOU'RE GROUNDED FOR THE NEXT SIX ROTATIONS. SPEND THE TIME IN THE SIMULATORS. WEDGE JUST PROGRAMMED SOME NEW SCENARIOS.
WHAT?
BUT I'M THE BEST PILOT YOU'VE GOT!
RIGHT NOW...
...WEDGE GETS THAT HONOR. WEDGE FOLLOWS ORDERS. WEDGE SPENDS HIS PERSONAL TIME WORKING ON TRAINING PACKAGES TO HELP KEEP HIS PILOTS ALIVE.
DISMISSED, FLIGHT OFFICER SKYWALKER.
sigh
THREEPIO?
YES, PRINCESS?
DISABLE LUKE'S X-WING COMMAND CODES UNTIL YOU HEAR OTHERWISE FROM ME.

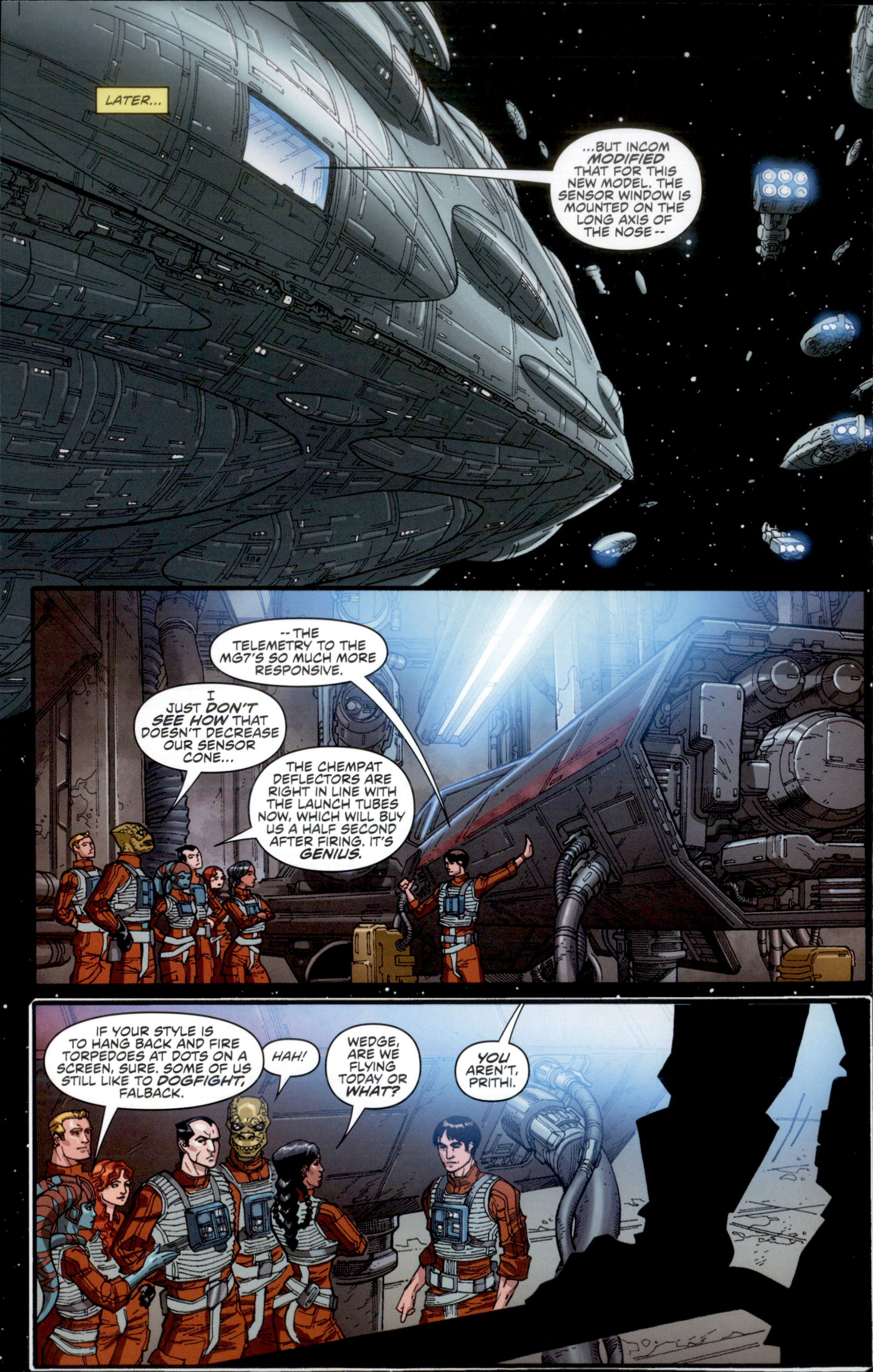
LATER...
...BUT INCOM MODIFIED THAT FOR THIS NEW MODEL. THE SENSOR WINDOW IS MOUNTED ON THE LONG AXIS OF THE NOSE--
--THE TELEMETRY TO THE MG7'S SO MUCH MORE RESPONSIVE.
I JUST DON'T SEE HOW THAT DOESN'T DECREASE OUR SENSOR CONE...
THE CHEMPAT DEFLECTORS ARE RIGHT IN LINE WITH THE LAUNCH TUBES NOW, WHICH WILL BUY US A HALF SECOND AFTER FIRING. IT'S GENIUS.
IF YOUR STYLE IS TO HANG BACK AND FIRE TORPEDOES AT DOTS ON A SCREEN, SURE. SOME OF US STILL LIKE TO DOGFIGHT, FALBACK.
HAH!
WEDGE, ARE WE FLYING TODAY OR WHAT?
YOU AREN'T, PRITHI.

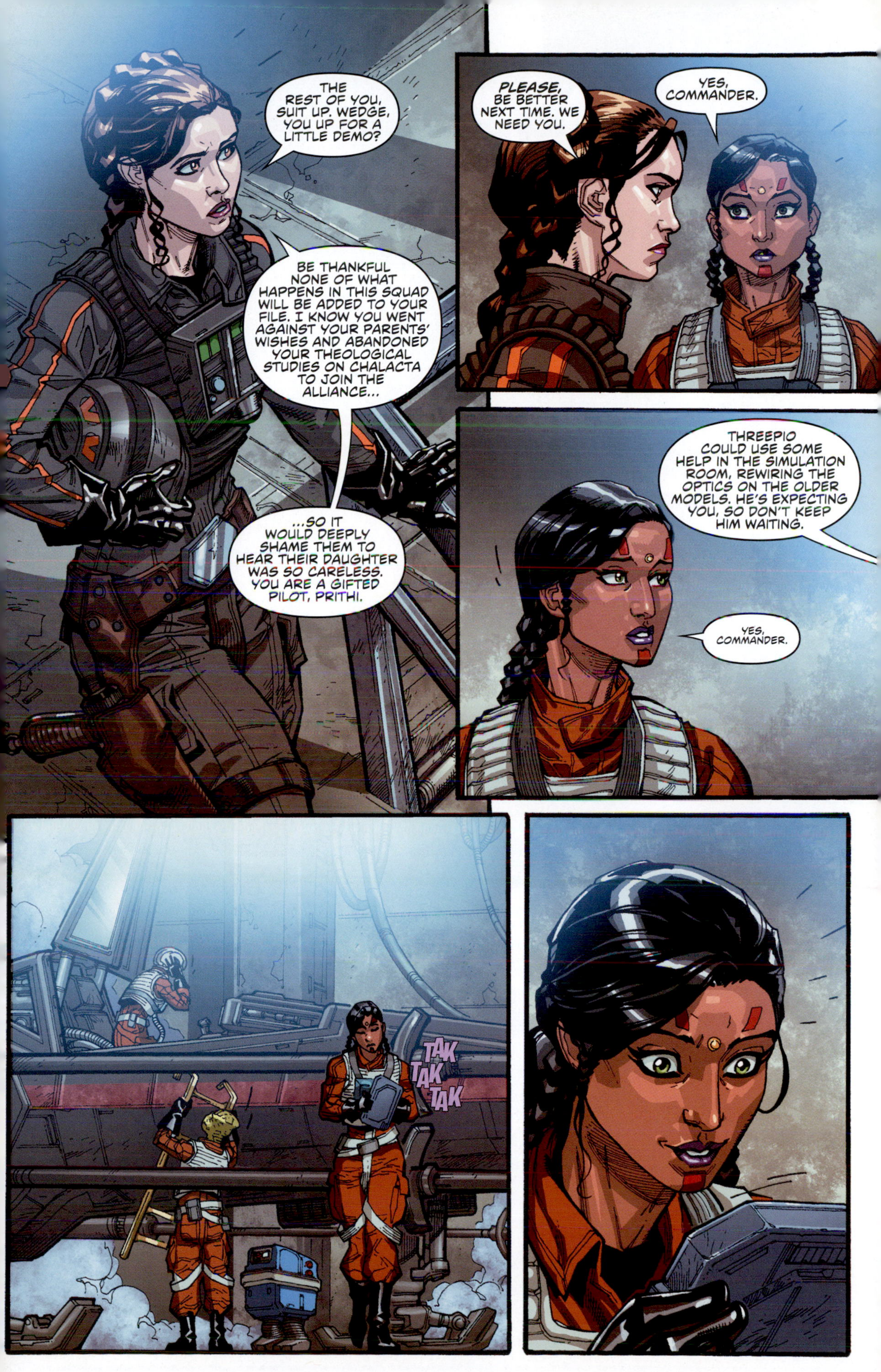
THE REST OF YOU, SUIT UP. WEDGE, YOU UP FOR A LITTLE DEMO?
BE THANKFUL NONE OF WHAT HAPPENS IN THIS SQUAD WILL BE ADDED TO YOUR FILE. I KNOW YOU WENT AGAINST YOUR PARENTS' WISHES AND ABANDONED YOUR THEOLOGICAL STUDIES ON CHALACTA TO JOIN THE ALLIANCE...
...SO IT WOULD DEEPLY SHAME THEM TO HEAR THEIR DAUGHTER WAS SO CARELESS. YOU ARE A GIFTED PILOT, PRITHI.
PLEASE, BE BETTER NEXT TIME. WE NEED YOU.
YES, COMMANDER.
THREEPIO COULD USE SOME HELP IN THE SIMULATION ROOM, REWIRING THE OPTICS ON THE OLDER MODELS. HE'S EXPECTING YOU, SO DON'T KEEP HIM WAITING.
YES, COMMANDER.
TAK TAK TAK

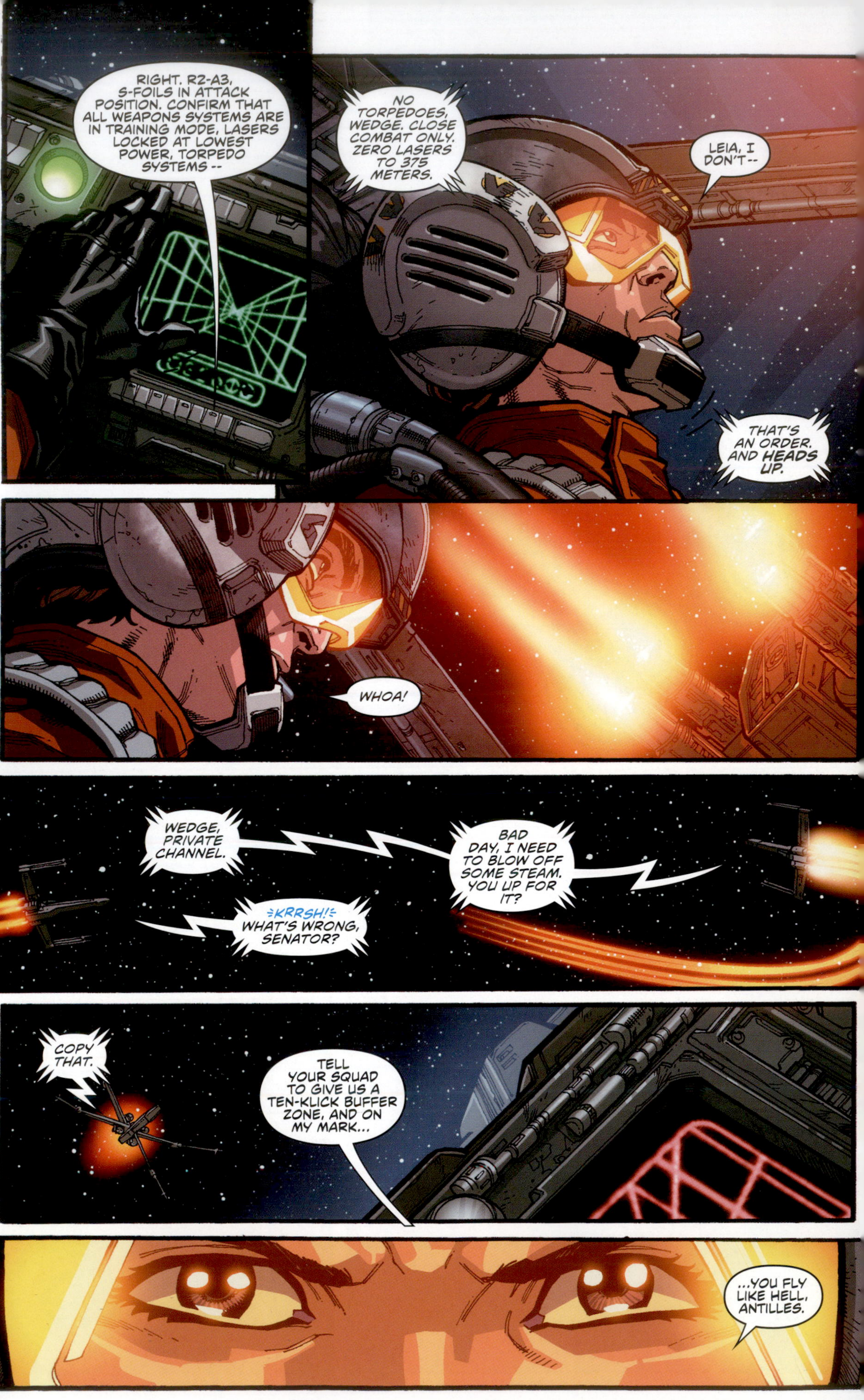

RIGHT. R2-A3, S-FOILS IN ATTACK POSITION. CONFIRM THAT ALL WEAPONS SYSTEMS ARE IN TRAINING MODE, LASERS LOCKED AT LOWEST POWER, TORPEDO SYSTEMS --
NO TORPEDOES, WEDGE. CLOSE COMBAT ONLY. ZERO LASERS TO 375 METERS.
LEIA, I DON'T --
THAT'S AN ORDER. AND HEADS UP.
WHOA!
WEDGE, PRIVATE CHANNEL.
BAD DAY, I NEED TO BLOW OFF SOME STEAM. YOU UP FOR IT?
KRRSH! WHAT'S WRONG, SENATOR?
COPY THAT.
TELL YOUR SQUAD TO GIVE US A TEN-KLICK BUFFER ZONE, AND ON MY MARK...
...YOU FLY LIKE HELL, ANTILLES.

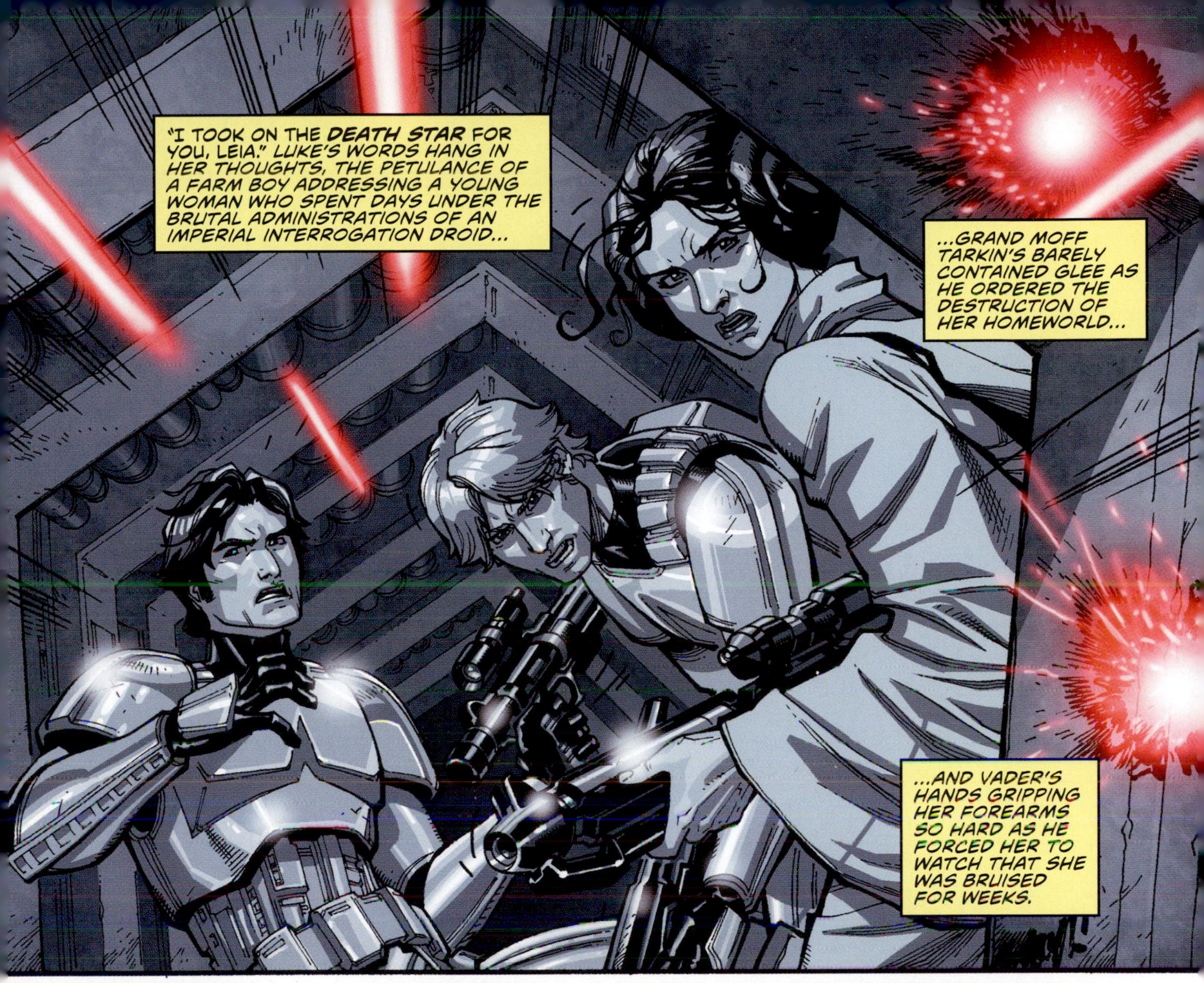
"I TOOK ON THE DEATH STAR FOR YOU, LEIA." LUKE'S WORDS HANG IN HER THOUGHTS, THE PETULANCE OF A FARM BOY ADDRESSING A YOUNG WOMAN WHO SPENT DAYS UNDER THE BRUTAL ADMINISTRATIONS OF AN IMPERIAL INTERROGATION DROID...
...GRAND MOFF TARKIN'S BARELY CONTAINED GLEE AS HE ORDERED THE DESTRUCTION OF HER HOMEWORLD...
...AND VADER'S HANDS GRIPPING HER FOREARMS SO HARD AS HE FORCED HER TO WATCH THAT SHE WAS BRUISED FOR WEEKS.

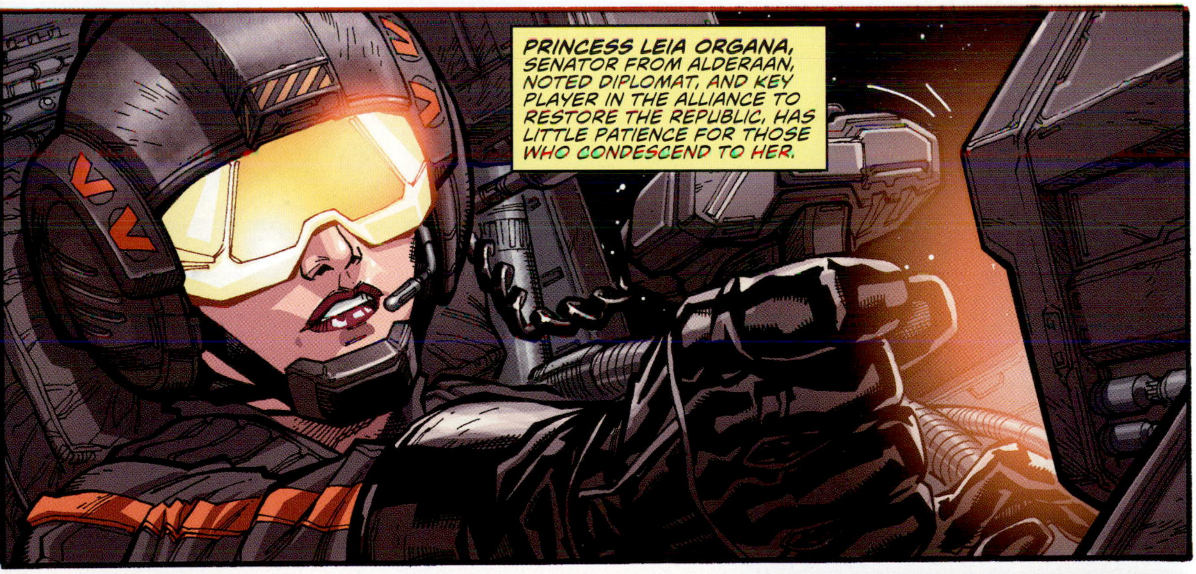
PRINCESS LEIA ORGANA, SENATOR FROM ALDERAAN, NOTED DIPLOMAT, AND KEY PLAYER IN THE ALLIANCE TO RESTORE THE REPUBLIC, HAS LITTLE PATIENCE FOR THOSE WHO CONDESCEND TO HER.

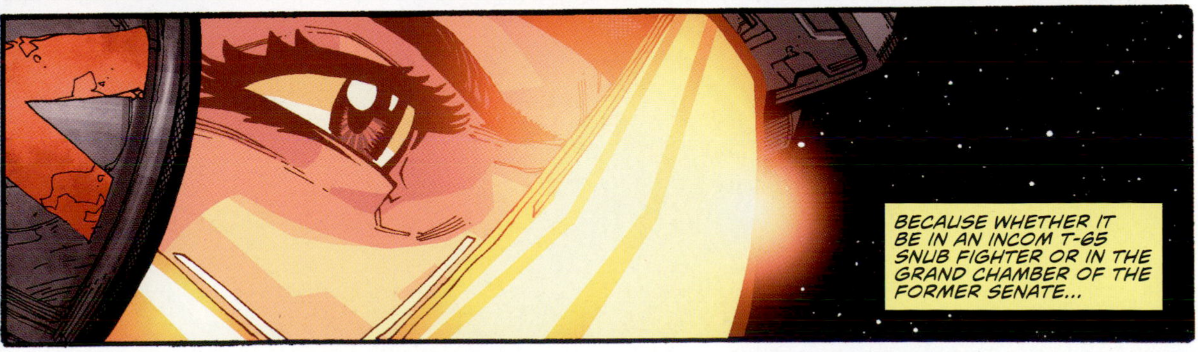
BECAUSE WHETHER IT BE IN AN INCOM T-65 SNUB FIGHTER OR IN THE GRAND CHAMBER OF THE FORMER SENATE...

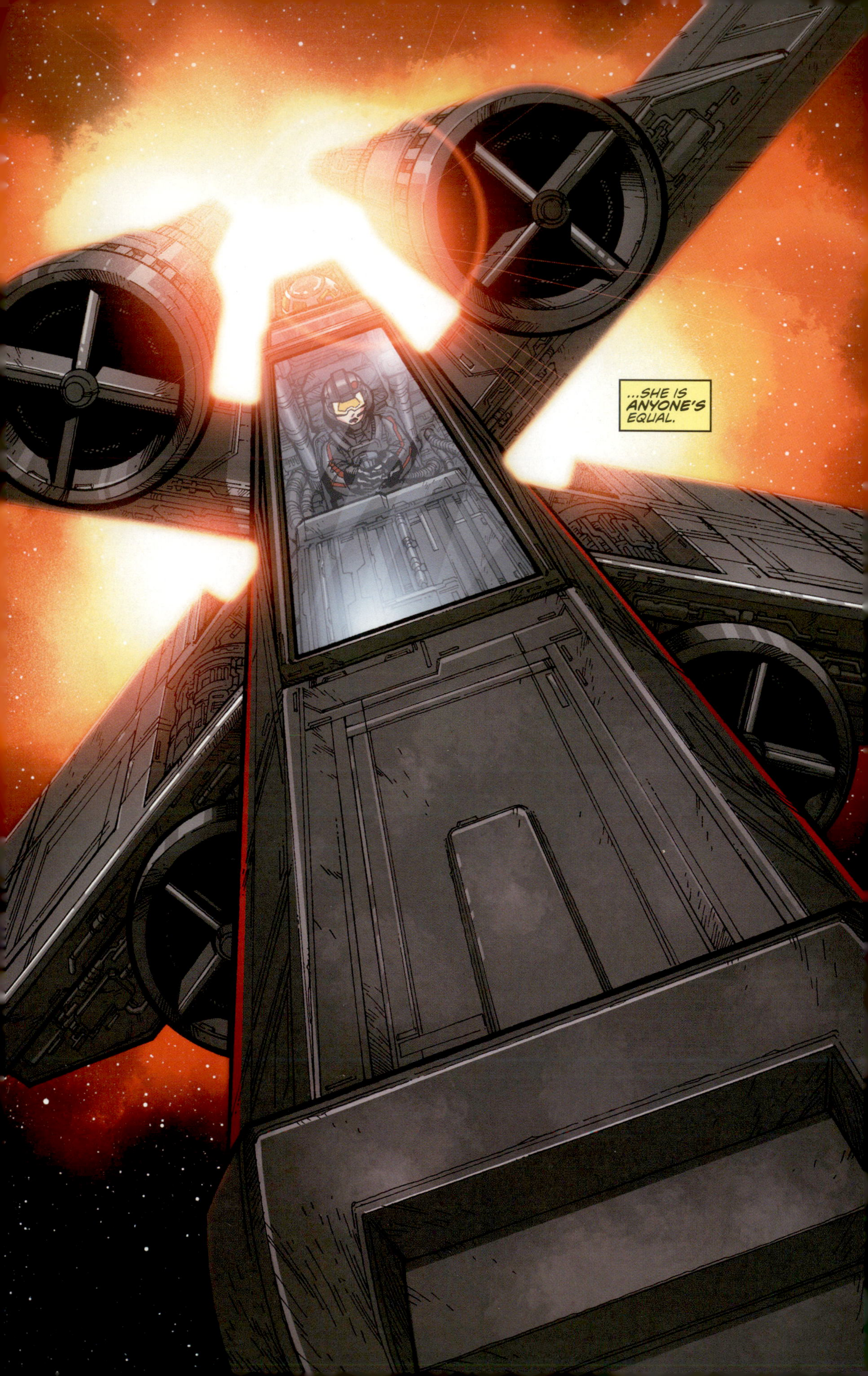
...SHE IS ANYONE'S EQUAL.

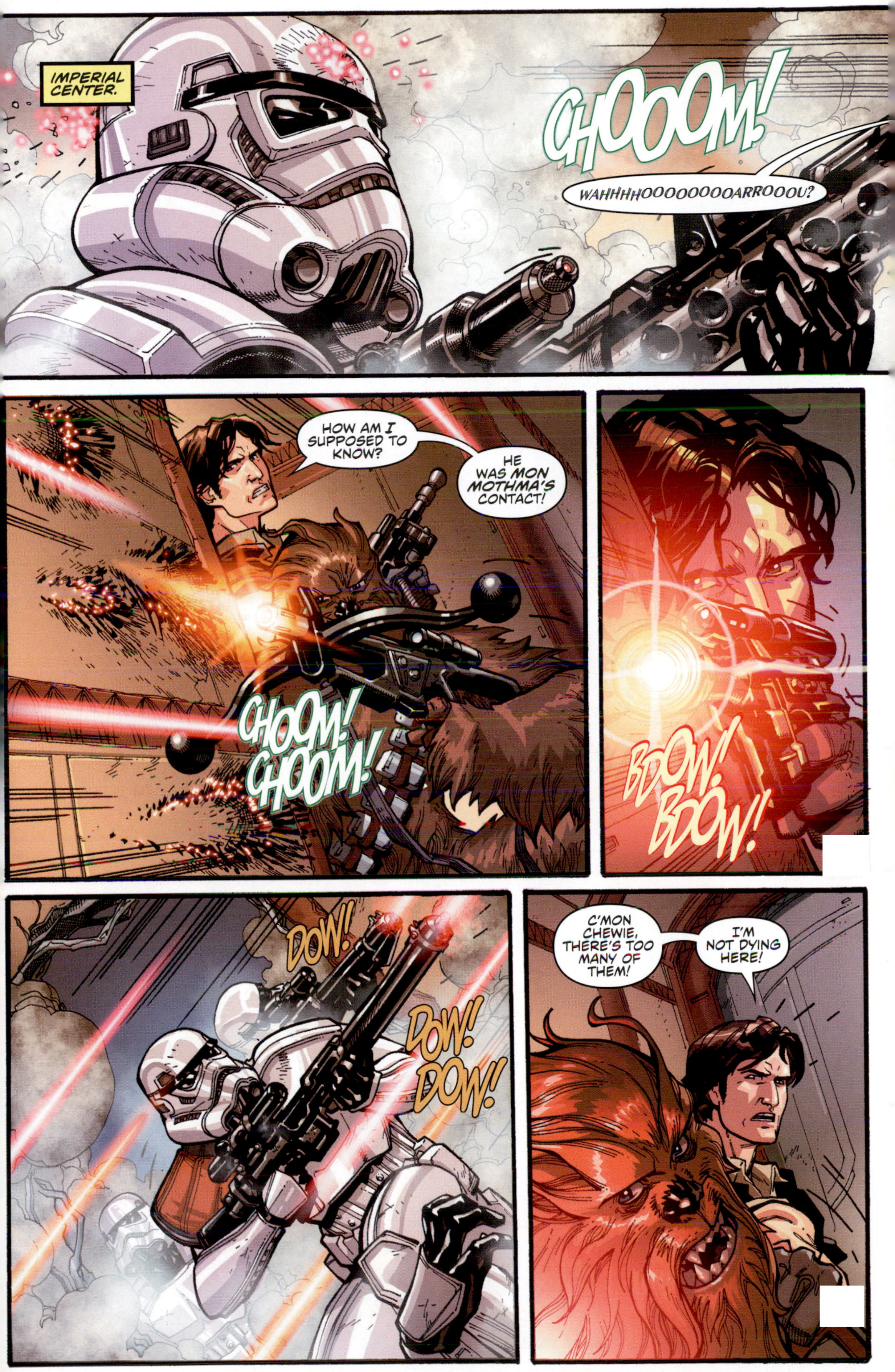
IMPERIAL CENTER.
CHOOOOM!
WAHHHHOOOOOOOOARROOOU?
HOW AM I SUPPOSED TO KNOW?
HE WAS MON MOTHMA'S CONTACT!
CHOOM! CHOOM!
BDOW! BDOW!
DOW!
DOW! DOW!
C'MON CHEWIE, THERE'S TOO MANY OF THEM!
I'M NOT DYING HERE!

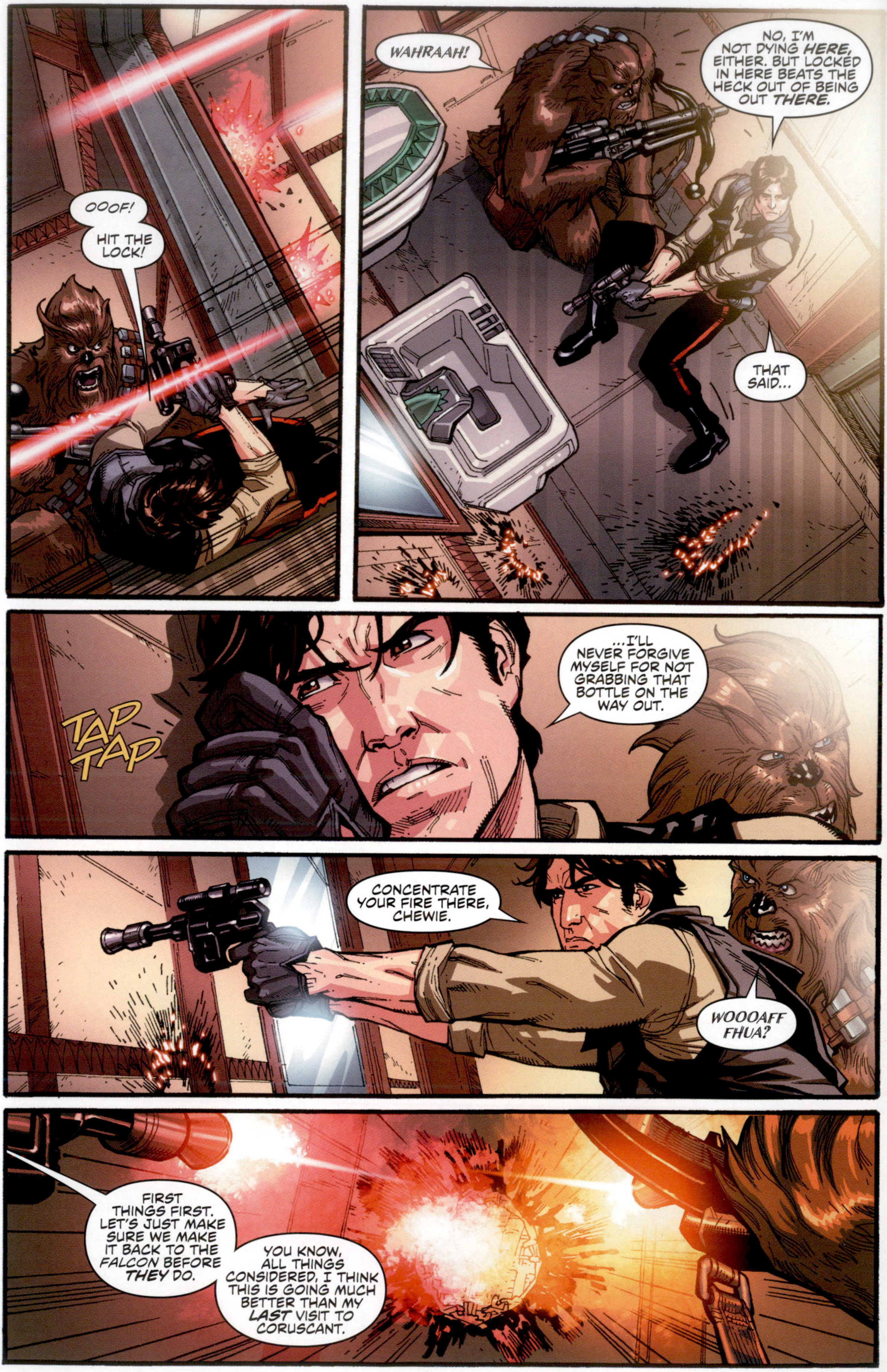
OOOF!
HIT THE LOCK!
WAHRAAH!
NO, I'M NOT DYING HERE, EITHER. BUT LOCKED IN HERE BEATS THE HECK OUT OF BEING OUT THERE.
THAT SAID...
TAP TAP
...I'LL NEVER FORGIVE MYSELF FOR NOT GRABBING THAT BOTTLE ON THE WAY OUT.
CONCENTRATE YOUR FIRE THERE, CHEWIE.
WOOOAFF FHUA?
FIRST THINGS FIRST. LET'S JUST MAKE SURE WE MAKE IT BACK TO THE FALCON BEFORE THEY DO.
YOU KNOW, ALL THINGS CONSIDERED, I THINK THIS IS GOING MUCH BETTER THAN MY LAST VISIT TO CORUSCANT.

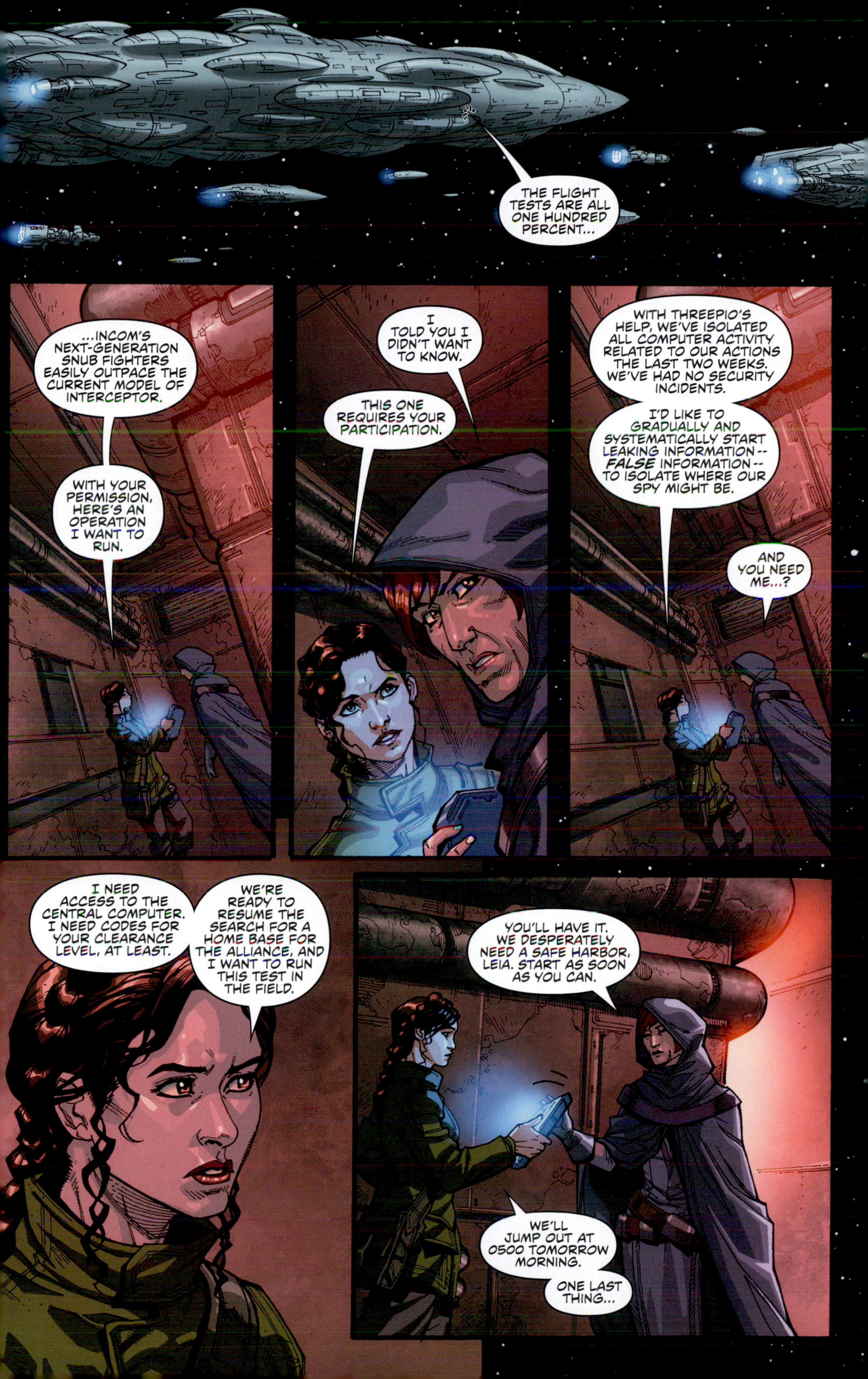
THE FLIGHT TESTS ARE ALL ONE HUNDRED PERCENT...
...INCOM'S NEXT-GENERATION SNUB FIGHTERS EASILY OUTPACE THE CURRENT MODEL OF INTERCEPTOR.
WITH YOUR PERMISSION, HERE'S AN OPERATION I WANT TO RUN.
I TOLD YOU I DIDN'T WANT TO KNOW.
THIS ONE REQUIRES YOUR PARTICIPATION.
WITH THREEPIO'S HELP, WE'VE ISOLATED ALL COMPUTER ACTIVITY RELATED TO OUR ACTIONS THE LAST TWO WEEKS. WE'VE HAD NO SECURITY INCIDENTS.
I'D LIKE TO GRADUALLY AND SYSTEMATICALLY START LEAKING INFORMATION -- *FALSE* INFORMATION -- TO ISOLATE WHERE OUR SPY MIGHT BE.
AND YOU NEED ME...?
I NEED ACCESS TO THE CENTRAL COMPUTER. I NEED CODES FOR YOUR CLEARANCE LEVEL, AT LEAST.
WE'RE READY TO RESUME THE SEARCH FOR A HOME BASE FOR THE ALLIANCE, AND I WANT TO RUN THIS TEST IN THE FIELD.
YOU'LL HAVE IT. WE DESPERATELY NEED A SAFE HARBOR, LEIA. START AS SOON AS YOU CAN.
WE'LL JUMP OUT AT 0500 TOMORROW MORNING.
ONE LAST THING...

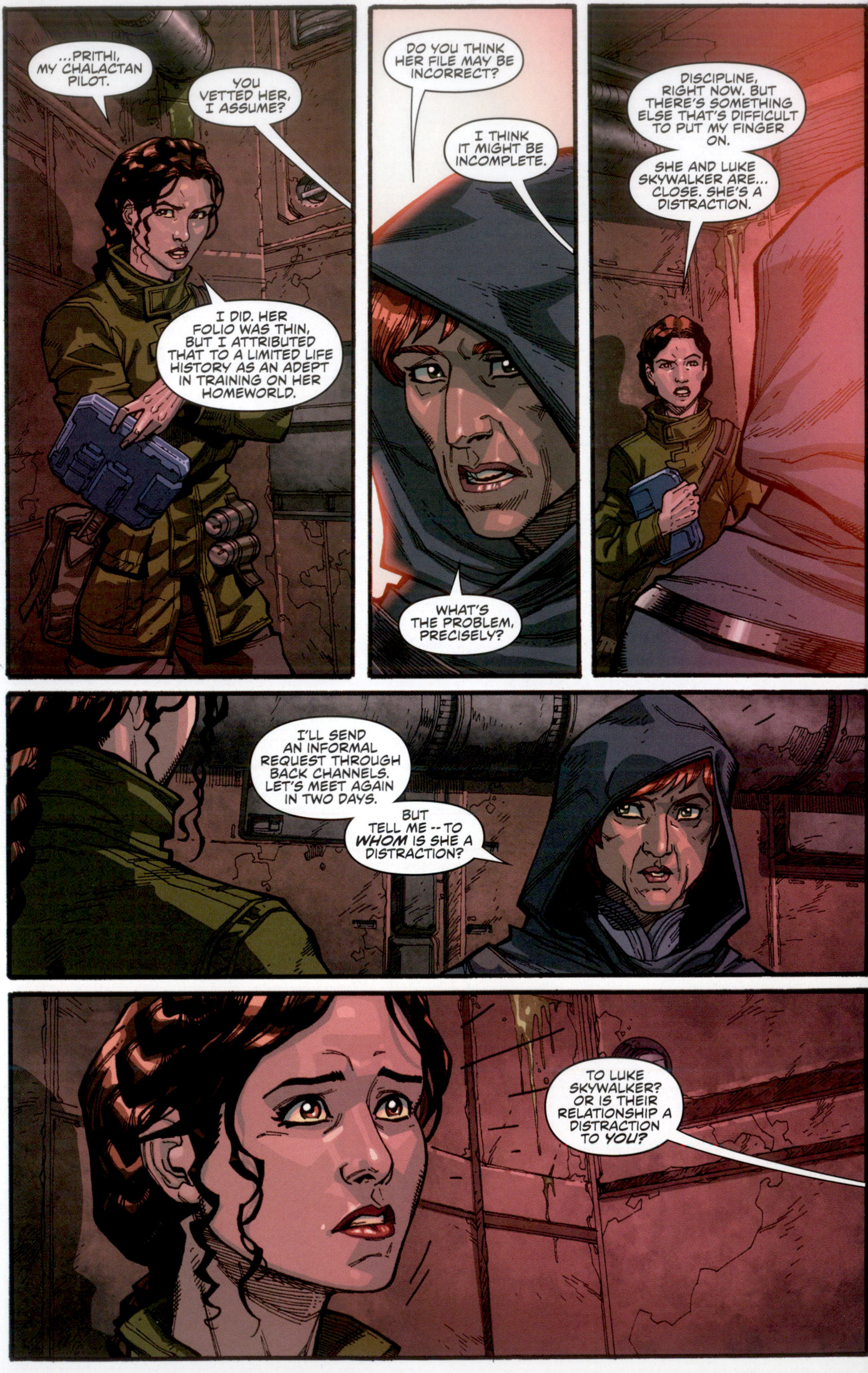
...PRITHI, MY CHALACTAN PILOT.
YOU VETTED HER, I ASSUME?
I DID. HER FOLIO WAS THIN, BUT I ATTRIBUTED THAT TO A LIMITED LIFE HISTORY AS AN ADEPT IN TRAINING ON HER HOMEWORLD.
DO YOU THINK HER FILE MAY BE INCORRECT?
I THINK IT MIGHT BE INCOMPLETE.
WHAT'S THE PROBLEM, PRECISELY?
DISCIPLINE, RIGHT NOW. BUT THERE'S SOMETHING ELSE THAT'S DIFFICULT TO PUT MY FINGER ON.
SHE AND LUKE SKYWALKER ARE... CLOSE. SHE'S A DISTRACTION.
I'LL SEND AN INFORMAL REQUEST THROUGH BACK CHANNELS. LET'S MEET AGAIN IN TWO DAYS.
BUT TELL ME -- TO *WHOM* IS SHE A DISTRACTION?
TO LUKE SKYWALKER? OR IS THEIR RELATIONSHIP A DISTRACTION TO *YOU?*

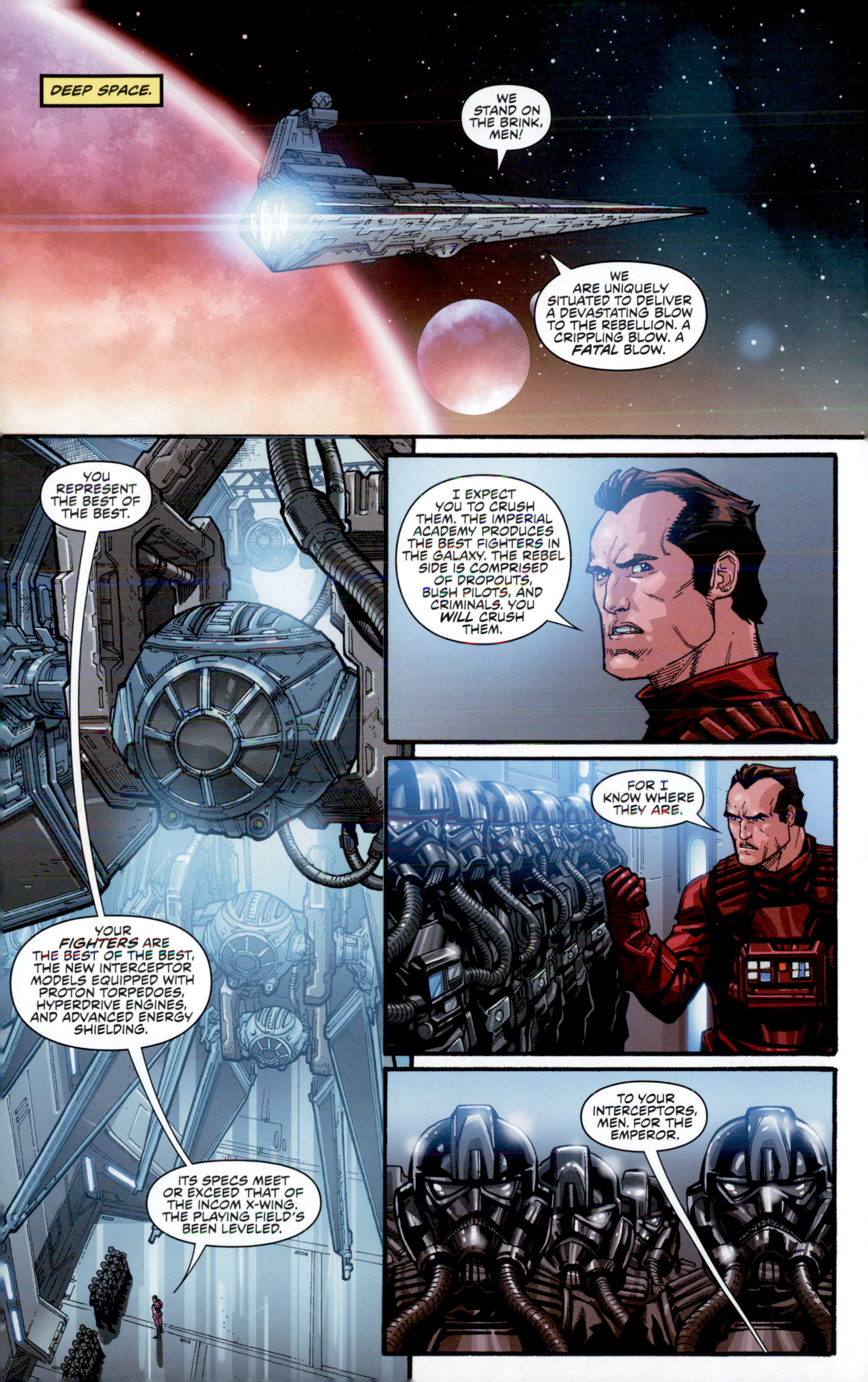
DEEP SPACE.
WE STAND ON THE BRINK, MEN!
WE ARE UNIQUELY SITUATED TO DELIVER A DEVASTATING BLOW TO THE REBELLION. A CRIPPLING BLOW. A FATAL BLOW.
YOU REPRESENT THE BEST OF THE BEST.
YOUR FIGHTERS ARE THE BEST OF THE BEST, THE NEW INTERCEPTOR MODELS EQUIPPED WITH PROTON TORPEDOES, HYPERDRIVE ENGINES, AND ADVANCED ENERGY SHIELDING.
ITS SPECS MEET OR EXCEED THAT OF THE INCOM X-WING. THE PLAYING FIELD'S BEEN LEVELED.
I EXPECT YOU TO CRUSH THEM. THE IMPERIAL ACADEMY PRODUCES THE BEST FIGHTERS IN THE GALAXY. THE REBEL SIDE IS COMPRISED OF DROPOUTS, BUSH PILOTS, AND CRIMINALS. YOU WILL CRUSH THEM.
FOR I KNOW WHERE THEY ARE.
TO YOUR INTERCEPTORS, MEN. FOR THE EMPEROR.

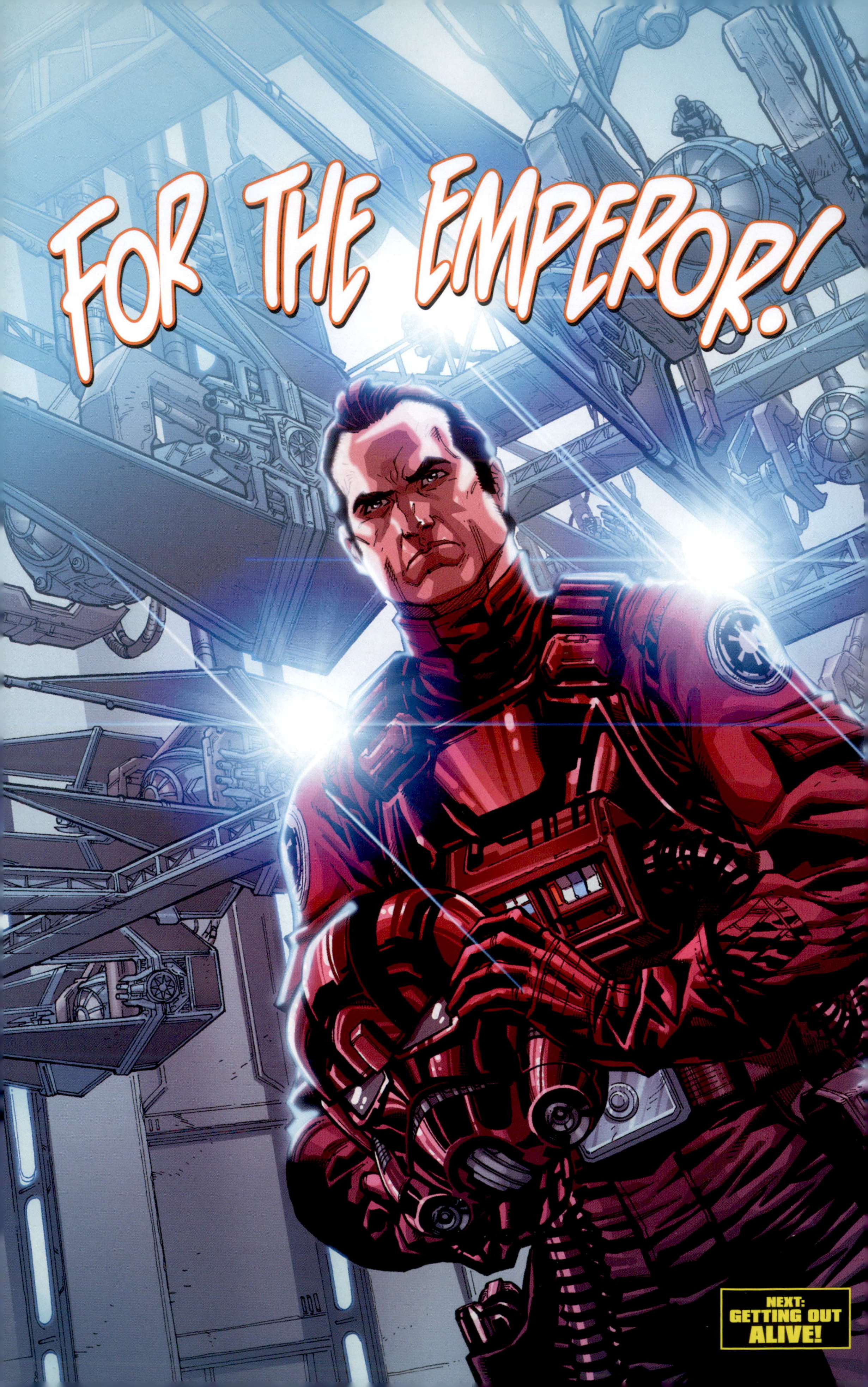
FOR THE EMPEROR!
NEXT:
GETTING OUT
ALIVE!